BEES + THINGS + FLOWERS

BEES + THINGS + FLOWERS

MICROFICTIONS

RAN WALKER

This book is a work of fiction. The names, characters, places and incidents are products of the author's imagination or have been used fictitiously and are not to be construed as real. Any resemblance to persons, living or dead, actual events, locales or organizations is entirely coincidental.

ISBN: 9781020001130 (Paperback)
ISBN: 9781020001208 (Ebook)

First Edition

10 9 8 7 6 5 4 3 2

www.45alternate.com
45 Alternate Press, LLC

CONTENTS

INTRODUCTION

What you are about to read is an experiment, an experiment in telling stories for which I am traditionally recognized and remixing them with a storytelling structure that I have heartily embraced over the past year and a half: microfiction.

Honestly, as I have read and reread these pieces, these "stories" have oscillated between feeling like prose poetry *and* microfiction. I attempted to create a seamless narrative, while simultaneously paying close attention to the language and how the words work together within that space.

In the end, such distinctions may not matter, except for how they are categorized on bookshelves. Here, though, is an expression that I liken to a *concept album*, that extended musical work that seeks to tell a collective, cohesive story over the course of its individual songs, albums like Marvin Gaye's *I Want You* and *Maxwell's Urban Hang Suite*.

I see the stories in *Bees + Things + Flowers* as working in concert with each other to tell a neo-soul "love" story. They are inspired by many different songs, the title itself coming from Roy Ayer's legendary, genre-defining song.

It is my hope that you will enjoy this story, as well as the form that I used to tell it.

Ran Walker
April 4, 2020

You don't love someone for their looks, or their clothes or their fancy car, but because they sing a song only you can hear.

— OSCAR WILDE

1

———

FIRST THINGS FIRST

"This is not a love story," she said.

"Good. I've never been big on those," he responded.

"But this still might hurt a little."

"Well, then make it hurt good."

AWARENESS

IT WAS the silhouette that started it all. Up until that point, he'd never paid attention to her.

But the light caught her lithe frame at an angle that created an inescapable gravity.

When he returned home from Queens, he couldn't stop softly humming her name, eager to touch himself.

3

______

LADY SOL

THE SECOND TIME he saw her was at a concert in Central Park. The sun seemed to be doing *the most*, kissing her skin and bathing her in this ethereal glow that made him want to shout, "Come on! For real?" All of this while Roy Ayers sang about the sunshine, bees, things, and flowers.

PLAYA PLAYA

HE USED their third meeting as an excuse to engage in a more endearing conversation. She welcomed his vibe—old school neo-soul, that it was.

Before long they were lying on the floor of his bedroom, smoking out, staring into the darkness of the ceiling, D'Angelo's *Voodoo* playing softly in the background around them.

YESTERNOW

HE HAD FELT her lips before in a dream he'd had when he was sixteen. She'd been a figment of his imagination then.

Now, incarnate, she took his lips and gently tugged those memories into her waiting mouth.

MF DOOM

NONE of his relationships in college had panned out, and he believed himself to be the blame.

But she didn't know that.

Maybe he could reinvent himself to be the man he knew he could be. After all, it was only a mask if you chose to hide behind it.

JOURNALING

SHE READ HIS WORDS, her hair brushing the prose of his notebook, her voice plucking each syllable and puffing them into the space between them.

The pen and paper, kindling. Her voice, the flame that set them both ablaze.

TRACK 1

"Be careful what you play," she whispered, as he turned on that first song. "This will be the soundtrack of our experience."

Experience. What an interesting word, he thought. But he was at a loss to find a better one.

ANALOG

IN THE FALL she'd head to some school in the midwest and he'd head down south to take a teaching job. But that was months away.

They remained oblivious to the sands sifting through the hour glass of their summer, content to avoid connecting on social media, choosing to keep their entire experience analog.

NO FEAR

SHE BROACHED THE SUBJECT FIRST, a flex to show she wasn't the scared type.

He was caught off guard, but his body responded to her wet whispers as they slid down onto his anticipation.

THICK

ACCELERATED, syncopated heartbeats.

The longing was too thick for them to play coy. They wanted each other: he her thickness, she his.

HUM

LATE AT NIGHT, as they whispered to each other over their phones, she would ask him to hum long and hard, then pretend she was holding the phone to her ear.

13

RAIN

IT RAINED the weekend she went out to Queens to visit her cousin. Occasionally he anthropomorphized the droplets on his window pane, imagining the shapes of *their* bodies undulating beneath the spray of a shower they had yet to share.

ACCENTUATED

"You're so country!" she said, laughing and resting her hand on his chest.

He'd tried to bury his accent in the vernacular of the city, but she'd seen through him.

Now he was completely vulnerable, but that no longer seemed like such a bad thing.

PUBLIC THEATER

THE SWEAT of sex still drying beneath his shirt, he realized the truest satisfaction of her body came when her fingers interlocked with his as they walked the streets of her neighborhood.

SEMANTICS

JOKING, he said, "We have a New York love affair with an L.A. soundtrack."

Nodding to Anderson .Paak, she smiled.

Later that night when she went home, the only part of his statement that continued to needle her was the "love affair" part.

RED LIGHT

SHE REMARKED that the red bulb he'd bought for the lamp in his room was corny, but the more her eyes adjusted, the more she realized how wrong she was.

It also didn't hurt that TLC's "Red Light Special" played softly on repeat.

BOOMERANG

ONE NIGHT she appeared at his door, cloaked in a trench coat and heels. She wasn't surprised when he answered the door wearing even less.

TIL THE COPS COME KNOCKIN'

THEY DIDN'T REMEMBER who'd come up with the idea of them locking themselves in his apartment all Saturday, making love, only stopping to sleep and nibble on Friday's leftovers.

On Sunday they awoke refreshed, had breakfast by the park, then kissed each other goodbye until Monday.

BATHING

THE BATHTUB WAS TOO small to comfortably hold them both, but that didn't stop them from trying. Water and bubbles sliding over the edge, extinguishing the tea candles, leaving them wet and alone in the dark, a feeling they were all too familiar with.

SONGS OF TONI

SHE WOULD LATER ADMIT to him that she'd fallen a bit harder for him because he had both versions of *Song of Solomon* on his bookshelf.

MUTHAFUCKIN' MOMENT

HER BODY MOVED in time with the strings, her fingers plucking pizzicato softly over his body, her arcane words burning into his soul, one syllable at a time.

A melancholy overtook him, as he knew it could never be this good again.

LOVE & BROWN SUGAR

HAND-IN-HAND, they navigated the labyrinth of Basquiat's mind, as Brooklyn hummed outside the gallery window.

They were a cliché of bougie Black love, but they couldn't help it. Each secretly wanted to be the lead in a romantic comedy from the aughts.

HOT NIGHTS

JULY WAS TOO HOT. Even breathing made him sweat.

At night, he slept with the window opened, the sounds of the city pouring into his room, swirling above his head like a fan, cooling him.

But then he'd think of her....

THIN LINE

IT WAS SMALL, slight, nearly imperceptible, but the shift had occurred.

As their bodies vibrated in the post-coital glow of orgasmic bliss, they had unknowingly crossed the line from having sex to making love.

INSECURITIES

ONE EVENING they stood entranced on the promenade, watching the sun set.

She wanted to ask him what would happen when the summer ended, but the moment was too perfect to fracture with her insecurities.

He struggled to suppress the words that bubbled in the back of his throat, the three words he felt too perfect to fracture with his insecurities.

MASSAGE

"YOU WERE one of those guys in college who used the excuse of giving a massage as a chance to shoot your shot, huh?"

"Wow. You have a low opinion of me," he said, laughing.

"I would have let you give me a massage," she responded.

"Really?"

"See, I knew you were that type!"

They laughed, as he continued to knead the warm oil into the small of her back.

SKETCHES

SHE CARRIED a sketch pad with her everywhere she went. Occasionally she'd find a bench, sit and draw the scenes of Fort Greene or Crown Heights or Park Slope or Bed-Stuy.

Before putting away her pencil, though, she would imagine him the way he appeared the last time she saw him and recreate that memory as best she could, unable to conceal her anticipation at seeing him again.

JIGSAW

SHE COULDN'T TELL how he was supposed to fit into the puzzle of her future. He was a splash of magenta contrasting against the achromatic tabs and blanks of her existence.

She wanted to ignore the future in favor of the present, blaming it on Zen, but every time their lips touched, she grew more and more afraid.

DESTINY, PART 1

THAT THEY WERE both in the city on internships for the summer could have been viewed by some as a coincidence, but they chose to view it as destiny, like The Jacksons' classic.

But, though neither would admit it then, they worried the albums that followed were better.

LOVE & WAR

IT WAS A DARE, that they could lie beside each other and not touch all night.

Each took turns trying to tempt the other: him humming in her ear, her singing softly in his.

He finally reached for his phone and played track three from *their* soundtrack (Janet Jackson's "Anything").

"That's not fair," she said, beginning to stir.

He smiled. "All is fair in—"

But she quickly placed her finger to his lips and replaced it with her tongue.

MAKE BELIEVE

NEITHER WERE REAL NEW YORKERS, but they playfully bantered about whether Harlem (where he was staying) or Brooklyn (where she was staying) was the dopest spot. Or maybe it was Queens, where they'd met. In the end, it hardly mattered, but for the moment they were cloaked in those costumes, so they decided to play the parts as they imagined such parts would be played.

ZAGAT

She carried a *Zagat* guide in her purse and picked a new restaurant for them to explore each week. Although she always offered to pay, he refused, paying for each excursion himself.

Eating leftover Chinese food and random pizza slices during the week , he didn't mind the sacrifice, just as long as he could marinate in the glow of satisfaction on her face.

WHY NOT

THEY LAY on their blanket in the park, her head resting on his chest, as they gazed at a skyline that attempted (but failed) to hide behind the trees.

Throwing logic to the wind, he thought, "Why couldn't this work? Distance is just an inconvenience these days, not a dealbreaker."

He said it over and over to himself, and when they made it back to his place Uptown, he almost believed it.

THE HEALER

FOR HER BIRTHDAY, he took her to see Fat Belly Bella. Afterwards they conversed about third eyes, true soul, Dilla, and hip hop, grateful that as the Earth continued to rotate and revolve, they were sharing that moment, knowing if it all stopped suddenly, they would go flying out into the universe together.

IN HER ABSENCE

IN HER ABSENCE, he would sleep diagonally across his bed, imbibing the lingering scent of her fragrance in the sheets, but saving just enough space that if she were actually there, his cheek would rest on her breast, her soft fingers dancing down his arm like a tiny ballerina pirouetting across the landscape of his body.

THIRSTY

HE DIDN'T envision himself the hugging type, but there was a way she embraced him that made him want to spend his days wrapped in her arms.

Even when they left each other after one of their many evenings across the city, he was always the last to let go, already thirsty for the next time their bodies would touch.

PALM

Sometimes they would meet in Times Square, her coming from the 2 train, him from the A train.

The would split a gummy bear and walk among the thousands of people, tethered together with warm hands, her index finger gently stroking his palm as a reminder of what would come when they were finally alone.

EARTH IS BETWEEN MARS AND VENUS

SHE FOUND it funny that they never argued. She'd never been with a guy where there wasn't some moment when personalities clashed. She couldn't determine if this was a good thing or not.

She wanted to find something in him that made it a necessity that things end with the summer, but she had yet to find that thing.

And before long, she gave up and gave in.

SLOW WINE

SHE'D BEEN LONGING to go some place and slow wine, so he found a place off Amsterdam that played dance hall.

He rested his hands on her rotating hips, meeting her gaze with his own.

When she nibbled seductively on her bottom lip, he found himself speaking involuntarily. "I want you."

She nodded and took him by the hand, as they danced out of the club and into the night.

MILES

WHEN HE WROTE ABOUT HER, he busted through the wall of clichés typically reserved for love poems, instead fixating on their experiences, the way Miles would enter into a private exchange with a musician on stage with him. There was no legend for the observer to translate the melodic magic embedded within the dialogue. It was personal. It was beautiful. It was theirs and theirs alone.

HEROES

ONE SATURDAY MORNING THEY SAT, curled up in the back of a comic book store in the East Village, talking about their inner superheroes. She was Riri Williams; he was Miles Morales.

It was only at the end of the summer that they realized they had both chosen teenage heroes. Maybe it was their last attempt to eschew the adulthood that awaited them in the fall, they silently wondered.

43

ANNIVERSARY

HE WASN'T the type to celebrate an anniversary that wasn't by definition a year long, but there was something about being around her that made him want to celebrate each day.

So when she invited him to come to her place for a one-month anniversary dinner, he ignored the denotative meaning, cued up Tony Toni Tone on his iPhone, and took his happy ass to Brooklyn with the quickness.

KILLING ME SOFTLY

IT HAPPENED at the end of a laugh, something random he'd managed to say to assuage his nerves.

Her mouth froze in astonishment. She had thought this would come, but hadn't allowed herself time to digest the thought, the implications.

His face flush with fever, he held her gaze, using the rest of his courage.

When she responded, "I love you, too," he was able to breathe again.

COMMON DENOMINATOR

Neither talked about what being in love meant or how it factored into their plans in the fall or what it meant for everything they did afterwards.

Now getting a slice of pizza was tinged in the brilliant hue of love. Holding hands. Kissing. Dancing. All, tinged in love. How would this new declaration affect them?

As they continued to enjoy their time together, they realized the reason it felt no different was because love had already been a part of the equation.

RIDING

IF THEY HAD BEEN in a city where driving was necessary, they'd have put on The Foreign Exchange's *Leave It All Behind* and taken a ride down the interstate.

Instead, they opted to snuggle on the 3 train, splitting AirPods and listening to *their* soundtrack as they glided through the belly of the island.

AUGUST

IN AUGUST, they sat facing each other with notebooks in their hands. She slowly sketched him, while he carefully composed a poem about her.

Once they finished, they exchanged what they'd created.

"You didn't sign it," he said.

"Neither did you," she responded.

"Maybe we should wait until, you know."

She nodded, slowly.

The end of summer was approaching and something as final as a signature could surely wait.

TOMORROW

With each "I love you," they drifted deeper and deeper into the other, their nude bodies wrapped so tightly at times they appeared to take on a single form.

With each thrust, they pushed away tomorrow, their exhalations like wind pushing a leaf into a backyard across town.

HOW DID WE GET HERE?

HE HAD GROWN up in Alabama and gone to college in North Carolina.

She had grown up in Nevada and gone to school in Ohio.

Both had been drawn to the allure of New York, having scouted internships that would let them experience what they'd seen in the favorite TV shows.

Love was never a part of their plans.

But now it seemed just about the only thing that really mattered.

PRETTY PETTY

THEY HAD their first argument two weeks before the summer ended. It didn't matter who'd started it or what it was about, but both figured it needed to happen.

Their fears had disguised themselves as pettiness, in an effort to find a clean exit from their relationship. But as the day drew on, none of it sat well with them.

He apologized. Then she apologized.

They were just no good at pretending to be mad at the other.

DISTANCE, PART 1

"HAVE you ever been in a long distance relationship?" she asked.

"No. You?"

"Once."

"How did it go?" he asked.

"Well, I'm here with you—and not him—right now. So there's that."

DISTANCE, PART 2

"You could fly up to see me, and I could show you around Chicago," she said.

"And then you could come spend spring break with me in Memphis," he responded.

"And there's FaceTime, too."

"True."

They needed to have this conversation—to show that they tried.

DISTANCE, PART 3

IT WAS his idea that they should finally add each other on social media and give FaceTime a dry run. So they decided to spend one of their precious remaining days trying their relationship remotely.

His phone felt foreign in his hands as he tried to send her videos and text messages. It felt unnatural, but he persevered.

At the end of the day, it was she who requested they meet face-to-face.

Phones resting by their feet, they embraced, sadness washing over them in heavy waves.

LAST TIME

THE LAST TIME they made love was the hardest. Neither wanted it to end, so they drew it out all night, collapsing into each other arms at dawn, neither of them having climaxed.

LAGUARDIA, PART 1

SHE WAS the first person to leave.

He rode with her in her Uber to the airport. The entire way they held hands in the backseat, searching for something profound to say to the other.

The words "thank you" felt too empty and insufficient. The words "I love you" were all that was left, its familiar refrain the end result of months of dialogue.

He got out at the airport and stood with her, as she awaited the security check.

"So this is it," she said, squeezing his hand.

He tried to communicate the world of his thoughts to her in their kiss, but unable to say anything further, he watched her leave.

LAGUARDIA, PART 2

HE TOOK the train to the bus and the bus to the airport. He had dreaded leaving the city, but that had changed after she left. Now he couldn't leave quick enough.

When she'd made it home safely, she'd texted.

He'd texted his relief that she was safe.

But there'd been no calls or texts since then.

When he boarded his flight and made it home, he didn't bother texting her to tell her he'd arrived.

MIXTAPES ARE FOREVER

A MONTH LATER, while listening to the radio, she heard one of *their* songs. It took her back to that small, neo-soul nook in Harlem, and she could feel his hands exploring her body all over again. The love was still palpable—which scared her.

She picked up her phone and stared at his number, willing herself to call him before the song went off.

But she never did.

DESTINY, PART 2

HE DIDN'T CONSIDER himself one who lurked on social media, but his fear had turned him into just that.

He knew her fall break was coming up, and he'd already booked his tickets to Chicago.

He didn't know what he would say to her when—or if—he found her, but like Michael Jackson sang on his *Dangerous* album, he couldn't "let her get away."

He smiled, thinking back to "Destiny" and realizing he was right all along.

SEARCHING

HE WAS SEATED in the food court when he saw her walk into the student union. He started to stand, fighting the weakness anchoring his feet.

Then he noticed the guy with her.

They weren't holding hands, but there was something in their glances, an intimacy, a *knowing*.

It was in that moment that he knew *their* experience was over.

He waited for them to pass, then slowly packed his things and left.

As he exited the building, he felt a soft hand on his shoulder, a familiar hand.

FOREVER EVER?

THERE WERE a million words and no words, so much to say and nothing at all.

Grant Park would never be Central Park, and Beale Street would never be Broadway. All they would have were those memories, triggered by songs and sunsets.

She thought of telling him how she'd waited, but there was no part of that plot that needed explaining.

Instead, they allowed themselves a final embrace, him trying to hold on to something he prayed was still there, her trying to return something dear that she was convinced she no longer needed.

FIRST THINGS FIRST REDUX

"THIS IS NOT A LOVE STORY," she'd once told him.

She was right about that.

Still, a part of him held on to hope, waiting until that space for her atrophied and gave way to a new experience with someone else.

But that would be a story for another time.

ACKNOWLEDGMENTS

I would like to thank my beautiful wife, Lauren, and my wonderfully inquisitive daughter, Zoë. You are the reasons I write.

I would like to also thank Torrey Walker, Sabin Duncan, Van Garrett, Nikki Williams, Mitchell Davis and the entire team at Biblio-Labs, and all of the librarians who continue to embrace me and my work.

Finally, I would like to tip my hat to Ana María Shua, Lydia Davis, Paul Strohm, and César Aira, inspirations for the form I used to write this book.

ABOUT THE AUTHOR

Ran Walker is the author of nineteen books. He is the winner of the 2019 Indie Author of the Year and 2019 BCALA Fiction Ebook Awards. He teaches creative writing at Hampton University and lives with his wife and daughter in Virginia. He can be reached via his website, www.ranwalker.com.

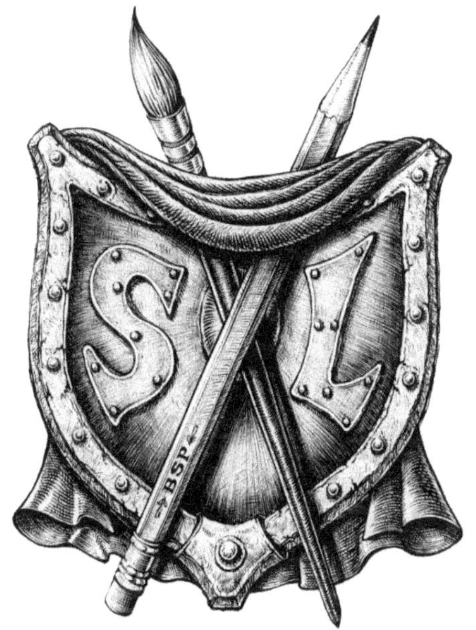

SKETCHBOOK LEGENDS

Book 1

A Collection of Short Stories
Written & Illustrated By T. Brown
Art Direction By Sherie L. Brown

BROWN SUGAR PRESS BOOKS

BROWN SUGAR PRESS BOOKS FOR YOUNG READERS is located in
Raleigh, NC 27616.

ISBN 978-0-9861203-9-8